KU-652-125

Ulf Nilsson ∽ Eva Eriksson

The best singer in the world

GECKO PRESS

EAST RIDING OF YORKSHIRE L.I.S.	
9016433988	
Bertrams	20/12/2012
	£10.99
COT	

I often sing to my little
brother. He loves it.
    First I sing *You Are My
Sunshine*, then *Jingle Bells*.
That makes him laugh
and bounce up and down
in his chair.

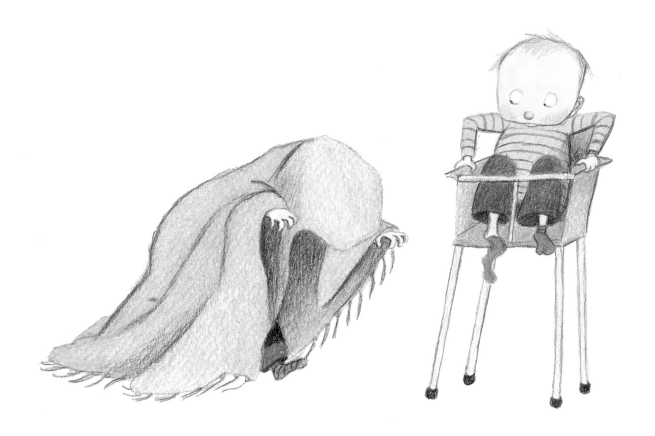

Then I pretend to be a prowling monster.
    But when I peep out and squeak, "It's only
me," he laughs so hard he's almost sick.

Best of all, he likes the song I made up for him.

My little brother's a wriggly piglet
Kiss 'em, tickle 'em…FART!!!

I kiss the air and tickle him, and when I sing, "FART,"
I blow a raspberry on his tummy so he rolls around
the floor laughing and shouting, "Again, again!"
 He thinks I'm the best singer in the world.

But I can't sing if there are too many people.

When I was six, we were having a performance at school to celebrate spring. It would be on a real stage, with proper spotlights. I told the teacher I didn't want to.

"I've got a good idea," she said. "You can sit beside the stage and only come out to tell us when the show's over."

I would just have to say a few final words, then there would be coffee for the parents and everyone would eat cake. But what costume could I wear? The only one left was a mole suit.

We practised hard. Everyone sang. When the rehearsal was over, I was meant to go on and say, "And now our little show has come to an end."

But I got really shy...

The teacher came with me
onto the stage. She said,
"You are absolutely the
best person for this very
important job."

I clung to her. The
spotlight shone in my
eyes. I said nothing. And
then I said...more nothing.
And then I said:

"Andnowourlittleshowhascometoanend."

Slowly, the lights went down. I stood there in the dark. The teacher said, "Tomorrow you can stand by yourself on the stage. And perhaps say the words a little louder and a little more clearly. You'll be a wonderful mole, you'll see…"

That night I couldn't sleep. On the stage all by myself. Speaking LOUDLY. Hall full of parents. Everything was terrible and my hands were all sweaty. What if I couldn't remember the words? It would be a catastrophe!

What if I just stood there with my mouth open? The parents would start throwing cakes at me. Then the school would get shut down and the teacher would lose her job. She'd have to go looking in rubbish bins for empty bottles to sell for money.

And me—what would become of me?

I rushed to Mum and Dad's bed and crept in beside Mum.

Would I be allowed in her bed after the concert? Would she even like me? I cried myself to sleep.

I dreamt that I was standing on the stage, and in came a monster, wrapped in a stinky old blanket.

Then it ate me up.

I couldn't eat breakfast. I couldn't eat anything. My hands were shaking so badly, I couldn't even drink.

"I can't wait to see your performance this afternoon," Dad said. "We're making a strawberry cake to bring with us."

"Shush," I said.

"Grandma's coming too," Mum said.

"Sing, sing!" said my little brother.

My stomach was in knots. "Sshh," I said.

I trudged off to school
after Dad. It felt like going
to prison. My stomach hurt.

At school, we made trees, flowers
and a big happy sun. We drew a pile
of dirt on a cardboard box to put
beside the stage. This was where the mole would
wait. We put out fifty-two chairs for the parents.
They were like waves in a great big ocean.

The stage was much bigger that day. It was like being at the edge of a cliff looking down at the sea. My heart was galloping. Mole alone onstage.

It was three o'clock—time to stand in my special place
behind the pile of dirt. I was the mole who would hear all
the spring songs and come up from the ground at the end.

All the parents had arrived. The hall was full.
There weren't enough chairs. Right up the back were
Grandma, Mum, Dad and my little brother. Everyone
was laughing and chatting.

Then a bell rang, and everything went silent. The
teacher went up on stage. Her shoes went click, clack,
click, clack.

"Welcome!" she said, loudly and clearly.

The curtain went up and all my friends were on stage.
A buzz went through the crowd. Cameras flashed.

My friends started to sing. They were amazing.

They sang, loudly and clearly. They stamped their feet at the right times. They waved their arms and smiled.

I was just a shy old mole in a pile of dirt. All I could do was mumble. What was I meant to say?

Something about a show and the end?

I was busting to go to the toilet.

I rushed out of the hall, right past the
laughing audience.

I got to the toilet and just managed to get my fly open in time. I didn't want to go back out. No way! I hid among the coats.

I'll be a mole forever, hiding from everyone, I thought.

"Little mole!" someone called suddenly. "Little mole!"

My brother was looking for me. I sat quietly among the coats.

I'll never, ever go onstage. I'll stay here alone in the dark, forever, I thought.

"Come out, little mole," he said. "Funny little mole!"

I peeked out. He laughed. "I see the little mole's nose!"
He sat beside me and held my hand. It was quite lonely
being a mole.

   I could hear them singing the last spring song.

   My little brother told me I was the best at singing.
"Best in the world! Sing, sing!" he said. He said he'd
come up onstage with his big, big big-brother.

   I sniffed.

I thought it would be pretty sad if I hid there in the coats and missed out on all the cake.

My little brother pulled my arm.

"I hate being scared," I said.

"Best in the world! Funny fart," my brother said. He poked my tummy and laughed. "Kiss 'em, tickle 'em! Come on, tickle 'em me."

I got up. We went into the hall arm in arm.

When the last spring song had ended,
we went up on the stage—one little brother
and a wide-awake mole with big claws. It was
absolutely quiet. I lifted the nose so I could look
out over the audience. I felt calm, as if the terrible
blanket monster had just let me go. I said:

"And now our little show has come to an end."

Someone started to clap, but then
I said:
  "That was the *little* end, but now
we'll have a few more songs. I'm
going to sing a funny one for my little
brother. It's his favourite. I made up
the words and the music myself."

  My little brother's a wriggly piglet.
  Kiss 'em, tickle 'em…FART!!!

"Again, again!" my little brother shouted.
   I started to sing our song one more time.
   My little brother's a wriggly piglet…
   I loved being on stage. I thought I'd follow
up with *Jingle Bells* and a joke, then I'd do the
Now-the-monster's-dead dance.

A wave of joy rose up inside me. I was ready to sing and dance for hours.

Kiss 'em, tickle 'em...FART!!!

My little brother rolled around on the stage, laughing.
Then slowly the lights went down. Out in the dark,
everyone in the audience was whistling and clapping.
    Then the ordinary lights came on.

The teacher came up and said she knew I would do it with pizzazz. She didn't think Grandma had properly heard what I sang.

Mum gave me a hug. She said I was very nice to my little brother. And that I was best in the world at singing.

Dad got a piece of cake each for me and my little brother.
We ate them.

Then my little brother sang the last line of our song.
Over and over and over again.